SUN AND SADDLE LEATHER
LEATHER
BY BADGER CLARK

PREFACE TO THE THIRD EL_____.

Cowboys are the sternest critics of those who would represent the West. No hypocrisy, no bluff, no pose can evade them.

Yet cowboys have made Badger Clark's songs their own. So readily have they circulated that often the man who sings the song could not tell you where it started. Many of the poems have become folk songs of the West, we may say of America, for they speak of freedom and the open.

Generous has been the praise given *Sun and Saddle Leather*, but perhaps no criticism has summed up the work so satisfactorily as the comment of the old cow man who said, "You can break me if there's a dead poem in the book, I read the hull of it. Who in H—— is this kid Clark, anyway? I don't know how he knowed, but he *knows*."

That is what proves Badger Clark the real poet. He knows. Beyond his wonderful [pg]presentation of the West is the quality of universal appeal that makes his work real art. He has tied the West to the universe.

The old cow man is not the only one who has wondered who Badger Clark was. Charles Wharton Stork speaking of *Sun and Saddle Leather*, said, "It has splendid flavor and fine artistic handling as well. I should like to know more of the author, whether he was a cow puncher or merely got inside his psychology by imagination."

Badger Clark was brought up in the West. As a boy he lived in Deadwood, South Dakota. The town at that time was trying to live down the reputation for exuberant indecorum which she had acquired during the gold rush; but her five churches operating two hours a week could make little headway against the competition of two dance halls and twenty-six saloons running twenty-four hours a day.

[pg]

Perhaps it was these early impressions that make *The Piano at Red's* in Mr. Clark's later volume *Grass Grown Trails* so vivid.

Scuffling feet and thud of fists,
Curses hot as fire—
Still the music sang of love,
Longin', lost desire,
Dreams that never could have been
Joys that couldn't stay—
While the man upon the floor
Wiped the blood away.

After Clark had grown up, in the cow country near the Mexican border, he stumbled unexpectedly into paradise. He was given charge of a small ranch and the responsibility for a bunch of cattle just large enough to amuse him, but too small to demand a full day's work once a month. The sky was persistently blue, the sunlight was richly golden, the folds of the barren mountains and the wide reaches of the range were [pg]full of many lovely colors, and his nearest neighbor was eight miles away.

The cow men who dropped in for a meal now and then in the course of their interminable riding appeared to have ridden directly out of books of adventure, with old-young faces full of sun wrinkles, careless mouths full of bad grammar, strange oaths and stranger yarns, and hearts for the most part as open and shadowless as the country they daily ranged.

In the evenings as Clark placed his boot heels on the porch railing, smote the strings of his guitar and broke the tense silence of the warm, dry twilight with song, he often wondered, as his eyes rested dreamily on the spikey yuccas that stood out sharp and black against the clear lemon color of the sunset west, why hermit life in the desert was traditionally a sad, penitential affair.

In a letter to his mother a month or two [pg]after settling in Arizona he found prose too weak to express his utter content and perpetrated his first verses. She, with natural pride, sent the verses to a magazine, the old*Pacific Monthly*, and a week or two later the desert dweller was astonished beyond measure to receive his first editorial check. The discovery that certain people in the world were willing to pay money for such rhymes as he could write bent the whole course of his subsequent life, for good or evil, and the occasional lyric impulse hardened into a habit which has consumed much of his time and most of his serious thought since that date. The verses written to his mother were *Ridin'*, the first poem in his first book, *Sun and Saddle Leather*, and the greater part of the poems in both*Sun and Saddle Leather* and *Grass Grown Trails* were written in Arizona.

Sun and Saddle Leather and *Grass Grown Trails* are books of Western songs, simple [pg]and ringing and yet with an ample vision that makes them unique among poems written in a local vernacular. The spirit of them is eternal, the spirit of youth in the open, and their background is "God's Reserves," the vast reach of Western mesa and plain that will always remain free—"the way that it was when the world was new."

Every poem carries a breath of plains, wind-flavored with a tang of camp smoke; and, varied as they are in tune and tone, they do not contain a single note that is labored or unnatural. They are of native Western stock, as indigenous to the soil as the agile cow ponies whose hoofs evidently beat the time for their swinging measures; and it is this quality, as well as their appealing music, that has already given them such wide popularity, East and West.

That they were born in the saddle and written for love rather than for publication [pg]is a conviction that the reader of them can hardly escape. From the impish merriment of *From Town* to the deep but fearless piety of *The Cowboy's Prayer*, these songs ring true; and are as healthy as the big, bright country whence they came.

In 1917, about the time our first edition of *Sun and Saddle Leather*began to run low, we fortunately discovered L. A. Huffman, of

Miles City, Montana, the illustrator who in 1878 began taking photographs from the saddle with crude cameras he made over to meet his needs. These same views were the first of the now famous "Huffman Pictures," beginning with the Indians and buffaloes round about Ft. Keogh on the Yellowstone where he was post photographer for General Miles' army during those stirring territorial days. The Huffman Studio is still one of the show places of Miles City, and the sales headquarters also for Montana and adjacent states [pg]for both of Mr. Clark's books, *Sun and Saddle Leather* and *Grass Grown Trails*. In a recent letter Mr. Huffman says, "I have just come back from a trip to 'Powder River' and along the Wyoming-Montana border. It's all too true! Clark saw and wrote it none too soon in *The Passing of the Trail*."

The trail's a lane, the trail's a lane.
Dead is the branding fire.
The prairies wild are tame and mild
All close-corralled with wire.
The sunburnt demigods who ranged
And laughed and loved so free
Have topped the last divide, or changed
To men like you and me.
[7]

SUN AND SADDLE LEATHER

[12]

[13]

RIDIN'

There is some that likes the city—
Grass that's curried smooth and green,
Theaytres and stranglin' collars,
Wagons run by gasoline—
But for me it's hawse and saddle
Every day without a change,
And a desert sun a-blazin'
On a hundred miles of range.
Just a-ridin', a-ridin'—
Desert ripplin' in the sun,

3

Mountains blue along the skyline—
I don't envy anyone
When I'm ridin'.
When my feet is in the stirrups
And my hawse is on the bust,
With his hoofs a-flashin' lightnin'
From a cloud of golden dust,
And the bawlin' of the cattle
Is a-coming' down the wind
Then a finer life than ridin'
Would be mighty hard to find.
Just a-ridin, a-ridin'—
Splittin' long cracks through the air,
Stirrin' up a baby cyclone,
Rippin' up the prickly pear
As I'm ridin'.
I don't need no art exhibits
When the sunset does her best,
Paintin' everlastin' glory
On the mountains to the west
And your opery looks foolish
When the night-bird starts his tune
And the desert's silver mounted
By the touches of the moon.
[pg]

"When my feet is in the stirrups
And my hawse is on the bust."
[pg]

[15]
Just a-ridin', a-ridin',
Who kin envy kings and czars
When the coyotes down the valley
Are a-singin' to the stars,
If he's ridin'?
When my earthly trail is ended
And my final bacon curled
And the last great roundup's finished
At the Home Ranch of the world
I don't want no harps nor haloes,
Robes nor other dressed up things—
Let me ride the starry ranges

4

On a pinto hawse with wings!
Just a-ridin', a-ridin'—
Nothin' I'd like half so well
As a-roundin' up the sinners
That have wandered out of Hell,
And a-ridin'.
[16]

THE SONG OF THE LEATHER

When my trail stretches out to the edge of the sky
Through the desert so empty and bright,
When I'm watchin' the miles as they go crawlin' by
And a-hopin' I'll get there by night,
Then my hawse never speaks through the long sunny day,
But my saddle he sings in his creaky old way:
"Easy—easy—easy—
For a temperit pace ain't a crime.
Let your mount hit it steady, but give him his ease,
For the sun hammers hard and there's never a breeze.
We kin get there in plenty of time."
When I'm after some critter that's hit the high lope,
And a-spurrin' my hawse till he flies,
When I'm watchin' the chances for throwin' my rope
And a-winkin' the sweat from my eyes,
Then the leathers they squeal with the lunge and the swing
And I work to the livelier tune that they sing:
"Reach 'im! reach 'im! reach 'im!
If you lather your hawse to the heel!
There's a time to be slow and a time to be quick;
Never mind if it's rough and the bushes are thick—
Pull your hat down and fling in the steel!"
When I've rustled all day till I'm achin' for rest
And I'm ordered a night-guard to ride,
With the tired little moon hangin' low in the west
And my sleepiness fightin' my pride,
Then I nod and I blink at the dark herd below
And the saddle he sings as my hawse paces slow:
"Sleepy—sleepy—sleepy—
We was ordered a close watch to keep,
But I'll sing you a song in a drowsy old key;
All the world is a-snoozin' so why shouldn't we?
Go to sleep, pardner mine, go to sleep."

5

"There's a time to be slow and a time to be quick."

A BAD HALF HOUR

Wonder why I feel so restless;
Moon is shinin' still and bright,
Cattle all is restin' easy,
But I just kaint sleep tonight.
Ain't no cactus in my blankets,
Don't know why they feel so hard—
'Less it's Warblin' Jim a-singin'
"Annie Laurie" out on guard.
"Annie Laurie"—wish he'd quit it!
Couldn't sleep now if I tried.
Makes the night seem big and lonesome,
And my throat feels sore inside.
How *my* Annie used to sing it!
And it sounded good and gay
Nights I drove her home from dances
When the east was turnin' gray.
Yes, "her brow was like the snowdrift"
And her eyes like quiet streams,
"And her face"—I still kin see it
Much too frequent in my dreams;
And her hand was soft and trembly
That night underneath the tree,
When I couldn't help but tell her
She was "all the world to me."
But her folks said I was "shif'less,"
"Wild," "unsettled,"—they was right,
For I leaned to punchin' cattle
And I'm at it still tonight.
And she married young Doc Wilkins—
Oh my Lord! but that was hard!
Wish that fool would quit his singin'
"Annie Laurie" out on guard!
Oh, I just kaint stand it thinkin'

Of the things that happened then.
Good old times, and all apast me!
Never seem to come again—
My turn? Sure. I'll come a-runnin'.
Warm me up some coffee, pard—
But I'll stop that Jim from singin'
"Annie Laurie" out on guard.
[22]

FROM TOWN

We're the children of the open and we hate the haunts o' men,
But we had to come to town to get the mail.
And we're ridin' home at daybreak—'cause the air is cooler then—
All 'cept one of us that stopped behind in jail.
Shorty's nose won't bear paradin', Bill's off eye is darkly fadin',
All our toilets show a touch of disarray,
For we found that city life is a constant round of strife
And we ain't the breed for shyin' from a fray.
Chant your warwhoop, pardners dear, while the east turns pale with
fear
And the chaparral is tremblin' all aroun'
For we're wicked to the marrer; we're a midnight dream of terror
When we're ridin' up the rocky trail from town!
We acquired our hasty temper from our friend, the centipede.
From the rattlesnake we learnt to guard our rights.
We have gathered fightin' pointers from the famous bronco steed
And the bobcat teached us reppertee that bites.
So when some high-collared herrin' jeered the garb that I was
wearin'
'Twas't long till we had got where talkin' ends,
And he et his illbred chat, with a sauce of derby hat,
While my merry pardners entertained his friends.
Sing 'er out, my buckeroos! Let the desert hear the news.
Tell the stars the way we rubbed the haughty down.
We're the fiercest wolves a-prowlin' and it's just our night for
howlin'
When we're ridin' up the rocky trail from town.
Since the days that Lot and Abram split the Jordan range in halves,
Just to fix it so their punchers wouldn't fight,
Since old Jacob skinned his dad-in-law for six years' crop of calves
And then hit the trail for Canaan in the night,
There has been a taste for battle 'mong the men that follow cattle

7

And a love of doin' things that's wild and strange,
And the warmth of Laban's words when he missed his speckled
herds
Still is useful in the language of the range.
[pg]

"We have gathered fightin' pointers from the famous bronco steed."
[pg]

[25]
Sing 'er out, my bold coyotes! leather fists and leather throats,
For we wear the brand of Ishm'el like a crown.
We're the sons o' desolation, we're the outlaws of creation—
Ee—yow! a-ridin' up the rocky trail from town!
[26]

A COWBOY'S PRAYER
(*Written for Mother*)
Oh Lord. I've never lived where churches grow.
I love creation better as it stood
That day You finished it so long ago
And looked upon Your work and called it good.
I know that others find You in the light
That's sifted down through tinted window panes,
And yet I seem to feel You near tonight
In this dim, quiet starlight on the plains.
I thank You, Lord, that I am placed so well,
That You have made my freedom so complete;
That I'm no slave of whistle, clock or bell,
Nor weak-eyed prisoner of wall and street.
Just let me live my life as I've begun
And give me work that's open to the sky;
Make me a pardner of the wind and sun,
And I won't ask a life that's soft or high.
Let me be easy on the man that's down;
Let me be square and generous with all.
I'm careless sometimes, Lord, when I'm in town,
But never let 'em say I'm mean or small!
Make me as big and open as the plains,
As honest as the hawse between my knees,
Clean as the wind that blows behind the rains,

8

Free as the hawk that circles down the breeze!
Forgive me, Lord, if sometimes I forget.
You know about the reasons that are hid.
You understand the things that gall and fret;
You know me better than my mother did.
Just keep an eye on all that's done and said
And right me, sometimes, when I turn aside,
And guide me on the long, dim trail ahead
That stretches upward toward the Great Divide.
[29]

THE CHRISTMAS TRAIL

The wind is blowin' cold down the mountain tips of snow
And 'cross the ranges layin' brown and dead;
It's cryin' through the valley trees that wear the mistletoe
And mournin' with the gray clouds overhead.
Yet it's sweet with the beat of my little hawse's feet
And I whistle like the air was warm and blue,
For I'm ridin' up the Christmas trail to you, Old folks,
I'm a-ridin' up the Christmas trail to you.
Oh, mebbe it was good when the whinny of the Spring
Had wheedled me to hoppin' of the bars,
And livin' in the shadow of a sailin' buzzard's wing
And sleepin' underneath a roof of stars.
But the bright campfire light only dances for a night,
While the home-fire burns forever clear and true,
So 'round the year I circle back to you, Old folks,
'Round the rovin' year I circle back to you.
Oh, mebbe it was good when the reckless Summer sun
Had shot a charge of fire through my veins,
And I milled around the whiskey and the fightin' and the fun
'Mong the other mav'ricks drifted from the plains.
Ay! the pot bubbled hot, while you reckoned I'd forgot,
And the devil smacked the young blood in his stew,
Yet I'm lovin' every mile that's nearer you, Good folks,
Lovin' every blessed mile that's nearer you.
Oh, mebbe it was good at the roundup in the Fall
When the clouds of bawlin' dust before us ran,
And the pride of rope and saddle was a-drivin' of us all
To a stretch of nerve and muscle, man and man.
But the pride sort of died when the man got weary eyed;
[32]

9

'Twas a sleepy boy that rode the night-guard through,
And he dreamed himself along a trail to you, Old folks,
Dreamed himself along a happy trail to you.
The coyote's Winter howl cuts the dusk behind the hill,
But the ranch's shinin' window I kin see,
And though I don't deserve it and, I reckon, never will,
There'll be room beside the fire kep' for me.
Skimp my plate 'cause I'm late. Let me hit the old kid gait,
For tonight I'm stumblin' tired of the new
And I'm ridin' up the Christmas trail to you, Old folks,
I'm a-ridin' up the Christmas trail to you.
[33]

A BORDER AFFAIR

Spanish is the lovin' tongue,
Soft as music, light as spray.
'Twas a girl I learnt it from,
Livin' down Sonora way.
I don't look much like a lover,
Yet I say her love words over
Often when I'm all alone—
"Mi amor, mi corazon."
Nights when she knew where I'd ride
She would listen for my spurs,
Fling the big door open wide,
Raise them laughin' eyes of hers
And my heart would nigh stop beatin'
When I heard her tender greetin',
Whispered soft for me alone—
"Mi amor! mi corazon!"
Moonlight in the patio,
Old Señora noddin' near,
Me and Juana talkin' low
So the Madre couldn't hear—
How those hours would go a-flyin'!
And too soon I'd hear her sighin'
In her little sorry tone—
"Adios, mi corazon!"
But one time I had to fly
For a foolish gamblin' fight,
And we said a swift goodbye
In that black, unlucky night.

10

When I'd loosed her arms from clingin'
With her words the hoofs kep' ringin'
As I galloped north alone—
"Adios, mi corazon!"
Never seen her since that night.
I kaint cross the Line, you know.
She was Mex and I was white;
Like as not it's better so.
Yet I've always sort of missed her
Since that last wild night I kissed her,
Left her heart and lost my own—
"Adios, mi corazon!"

[36]

THE BUNK-HOUSE ORCHESTRA

Wrangle up your mouth-harps, drag your banjo out,
Tune your old guitarra till she twangs right stout,
For the snow is on the mountains and the wind is on the plain,
But we'll cut the chimney's moanin' with a livelier refrain.
Shinin' 'dobe fireplace, shadows on the wall—
(See old Shorty's friv'lous toes a-twitchin' at the call!)
It's the best grand high that there is within the law
When seven jolly punchers tackle "Turkey in the Straw."
Freezy was the day's ride, lengthy was the trail,
Ev'ry steer was haughty with a high arched tail,
But we held 'em and we shoved 'em, for our longin' hearts were
tried
By a yearnin' for tobacker and our dear fireside.
Swing 'er into stop-time, don't you let 'er droop!
(You're about as tuneful as a coyote with the croup!)
Ay, the cold wind bit when we drifted down the draw,
But we drifted on to comfort and to "Turkey in the Straw."
Snarlin' when the rain whipped, cussin' at the ford—
Ev'ry mile of twenty was a long discord,
But the night is brimmin' music and its glory is complete
When the eye is razzle-dazzled by the flip o' Shorty's feet!
Snappy for the dance, now, fill she up and shoots!
(Don't he beat the devil's wife for jiggin' in 'is boots?)
Shorty got throwed high and we laughed till he was raw,
But tonight he's done forgot it prancin' "Turkey in the Straw."
Rainy dark or firelight, bacon rind or pie,
Livin' is a luxury that don't come high;

Oh, be happy and onruly while our years and luck allow,
For we all must die or marry less than forty years from now!
Lively on the last turn! lope 'er to the death!
(Reddy's soul is willin' but he's gettin' short o' breath.)
Ay, the storm wind sings and old trouble sucks his paw
When we have an hour of firelight set to "Turkey in the Straw!"
[40]

THE OUTLAW

When my rope takes hold on a two-year-old,
By the foot or the neck or the horn,
He kin plunge and fight till his eyes go white
But I'll throw him as sure as you're born.
Though the taut ropes sing like a banjo string
And the latigoes creak and strain,
Yet I got no fear of an outlaw steer
And I'll tumble him on the plain.
For a man is a man, but a steer is a beast,
And the man is the boss of the herd,
And each of the bunch, from the biggest to least,
Must come down when he says the word.
[pg]

"The taut ropes sing like a banjo string
And the latigoes creak and strain."
[pg]

[41]
When my leg swings 'cross on an outlaw hawse
And my spurs clinch into his hide,
He kin r'ar and pitch over hill and ditch,
But wherever he goes I'll ride.
Let 'im spin and flop like a crazy top
Or flit like a wind-whipped smoke,
But he'll know the feel of my rowelled heel
Till he's happy to own he's broke.
For a man is a man and a hawse is a brute,
And the hawse may be prince of his clan
But he'll bow to the bit and the steel-shod boot
And own that his boss is the man.
When the devil at rest underneath my vest

12

Gets up and begins to paw
And my hot tongue strains at its bridle reins,
Then I tackle the real outlaw.
When I get plumb riled and my sense goes wild
And my temper is fractious growed,
If he'll hump his neck just a triflin' speck,
Then it's dollars to dimes I'm throwed.
For a man is a man, but he's partly a beast.
He kin brag till he makes you deaf,
But the one lone brute, from the west to the east,
That he kaint quite break is himse'f.
[43]

THE LEGEND OF BOASTFUL BILL

At a roundup on the Gily,
One sweet mornin' long ago,
Ten of us was throwed right freely
By a hawse from Idaho.
And we thought he'd go-a-beggin'
For a man to break his pride
Till, a-hitchin' up one leggin,
Boastful Bill cut loose and cried—
"I'm a on'ry proposition for to hurt;
I fulfil my earthly mission with a quirt;
I kin ride the highest liver
'Tween the Gulf and Powder River,
And I'll break this thing as easy as I'd flirt."
So Bill climbed the Northern Fury
And they mangled up the air
Till a native of Missouri
Would have owned his brag was fair.
Though the plunges kep' him reelin'
And the wind it flapped his shirt,
Loud above the hawse's squealin'
We could hear our friend assert
"I'm the one to take such rakin's as a joke.
Some one hand me up the makin's of a smoke!
If you think my fame needs bright'nin'
W'y, I'll rope a streak of lightnin'
And I'll cinch 'im up and spur 'im till he's broke."
Then one caper of repulsion
Broke that hawse's back in two.

13

Cinches snapped in the convulsion;
Skyward man and saddle flew.
Up he mounted, never laggin',
While we watched him through our tears,
And his last thin bit of braggin'
Came a-droppin' to our ears.
"If you'd ever watched my habits very close
You would know I've broke such rabbits by the gross.
I have kep' my talent hidin';
I'm too good for earthly ridin'
And I'm off to bust the lightnin's,—Adios!"
Years have gone since that ascension.
Boastful Bill ain't never lit,
So we reckon that he's wrenchin'
Some celestial outlaw's bit.
When the night rain beats our slickers
And the wind is swift and stout
And the lightnin' flares and flickers,
We kin sometimes hear him shout—
"I'm a bronco-twistin' wonder on the fly;
I'm the ridin' son-of-thunder of the sky.
Hi! you earthlin's, shut your winders
While we're rippin' clouds to flinders.
If this blue-eyed darlin' kicks at you, you die!"
Stardust on his chaps and saddle,
Scornful still of jar and jolt,
He'll come back some day, astraddle
Of a bald-faced thunderbolt.
And the thin-skinned generation
Of that dim and distant day
Sure will stare with admiration
When they hear old Boastful say—
"I was first, as old rawhiders all confessed.
Now I'm last of all rough riders, and the best.
Huh! you soft and dainty floaters,
With your a'roplanes and motors—
Huh! are you the great grandchildren of the West!"
[48]

THE TIED MAVERICK

Lay on the iron! the tie holds fast
And my wild record closes.

14

This maverick is down at last
Just roped and tied with roses.
And one small girl's to blame for it,
Yet I don't fight with shame for it—
Lay on the iron; I'm game for it,
Just roped and tied with roses.
I loped among the wildest band
Of saddle-hatin' winners—
Gay colts that never felt a brand
And scarred old outlaw sinners.
The wind was rein and guide to us;
The world was pasture wide to us
And our wild name was pride to us—
High headed bronco sinners!
So, loose and light we raced and fought
And every range we tasted,
But now, since I'm corralled and caught,
I know them days were wasted.
From now, the all-day gait for me,
The trail that's hard but straight for me,
For down that trail, who'll wait for me!
Ay! them old days were wasted!
But though I'm broke, I'll never be
A saddle-marked old groaner,
For never worthless bronc like me
Got such a gentle owner.
There could be colt days glad as mine
Or outlaw runs as mad as mine
Or rope-flung falls as bad as mine,
But never such an owner.
Lay on the iron, and lay it red!
I'll take it kind and clever.
Who wouldn't hold a prouder head
To wear that mark forever?
I'll never break and stray from her;
I'd starve and die away from her.
Lay on the iron—it's play from her—
And brand me hers forever!
[51]

A ROUNDUP LULLABY

Desert blue and silver in the still moonshine,

15

Coyote yappin' lazy on the hill,
Sleepy winks of lightnin' down the far sky line,
Time for millin' cattle to be still.
So—o now, the lightnin's far away,
The coyote's nothiny skeery;
He's singin' to his dearie—
Hee—ya, tammalalleday!
Settle down, you cattle, till the mornin'.
Nothin' out the hazy range that you folks need,
Nothin' we kin see to take your eye.
Yet we got to watch you or you'd all stampede,
Plungin' down some 'royo bank to die.
So—o, now, for still the shadows stay;
The moon is slow and steady;
The sun comes when he's ready.
Hee—ya, tammalalleday!
No use runnin' out to meet the mornin'.
Cows and men are foolish when the light grows dim,
Dreamin' of a land too far to see.
There, you dream, is wavin' grass and streams that brim
And it often seems the same to me.
So—o, now, for dreams they never pay.
The dust it keeps us blinkin',
We're seven miles from drinkin'.
Hee—ya, tammalalleday!
But we got to stand it till the mornin'.
Mostly it's a moonlight world our trail winds through.
Kaint see much beyond our saddle horns.
Always far away is misty silver-blue;
Always underfoot it's rocks and thorns.
So—o, now. It must be this away—
The lonesome owl a-callin',
The mournful coyote squallin'.
Hee—ya, tammalalleday!
Mockin-birds don't sing until the mornin'.
Always seein' 'wayoff dreams of silver-blue,
Always feelin' thorns that slab and sting.
Yet stampedin' never made a dream come true,
So I ride around myself and sing.
So—o, now, a man has got to stay,
A-likin' or a-hatin',
But workin' on and waitin'.
Hee—ya, tammalalleday!
All of us are waitin' for the mornin'.

THE TRAIL O' LOVE

My love was swift and slender
As an antelope at play,
And her eyes were gray and tender
As the east at break o' day,
And I sure was shaky hearted
And her flower face was pale
On that silver night we parted,
When I sang along the trail:
Forever—forever—
Oh, moon above the pine,
Like the matin' birds in Springtime,
I will twitter while you shine.
Rich as ore with gold a-glowin',
Sweet as sparklin' springs a-flowin',
Strong as redwoods ever growin',
So will be this love o' mine.
I rode across the river
And beyond the far divide,
Till the echo of "forever"
Staggered faint behind and died.
For the long trail smiled and beckoned
And the free wind blowed so sweet,
That life's gayest tune, I reckoned,
Was my hawse's ringin' feet.
Forever—forever—
Oh, stars, look down and sigh,
For a poison spring will sparkle
And the trustin' drinker die.
And a rovin' bird will twitter
And a worthless rock will glitter
And the maiden's love is bitter
When the man's is proved a lie.
Last the rover's circle guidin'
Brought me where I used to be,
And I met her, gaily ridin'
With a smarter man than me.
Then I raised my dusty cover
But she didn't see nor hear,
So I hummed the old tune over,

17

Laughin' in my hawse's ear:
If the snowflake specks the desert
Or the yucca blooms awhile.
Ay! what gloom the mountain covers
Where the driftin' cloud shade hovers!
Ay! the trail o' parted lovers,
Where "forever" lasts a mile!
[58]

BACHIN'

Our lives are hid; our trails are strange;
We're scattered through the West
In canyon cool, on blistered range
Or windy mountain crest.
Wherever Nature drops her ears
And bares her claws to scratch,
From Yuma to the north frontiers,
You'll likely find the bach',
You will,
The shy and sober bach'!
Our days are sun and storm and mist,
The same as any life,
Except that in our trouble list
We never count a wife.
Each has a reason why he's lone,
But keeps it 'neath his hat;
Or, if he's got to tell some one,
Confides it to his cat,
He does,
Just tells it to his cat.
We're young or old or slow or fast,
But all plumb versatyle.
The mighty bach' that fires the blast
Kin serve up beans in style.
The bach' that ropes the plungin' cows
Kin mix the biscuits true—
We earn our grub by drippin' brows
And cook it by 'em too,
We do,
We cook it by 'em too.
We like to breathe unbranded air,
Be free of foot and mind,

18

And go or stay, or sing or swear,
Whichever we're inclined.
An appetite, a conscience clear,
A pipe that's rich and old
Are loves that always bless and cheer
And never cry nor scold,
They don't.
They never cry nor scold.
Old Adam bached some ages back
And smoked his pipe so free,
A-loafin' in a palm-leaf shack
Beneath a mango tree.
He'd best have stuck to bachin' ways,
And scripture proves the same,
For Adam's only happy days
Was 'fore the woman came,
They was,
All 'fore the woman came.
[61]

THE GLORY TRAIL

'Way high up the Mogollons,
Among the mountain tops,
A lion cleaned a yearlin's bones
And licked his thankful chops,
When on the picture who should ride,
A-trippin' down a slope,
But High-Chin Bob, with sinful pride
And mav'rick-hungry rope.
"Oh, glory be to me," says he,
"And fame's unfadin' flowers!
All meddlin' hands are far away;
I ride my good top-hawse today
And I'm top-rope of the Lazy J——
Hi! kitty cat, you're ours!"
That lion licked his paw so brown
And dreamed soft dreams of veal—
And then the circlin' loop sung down
And roped him 'round his meal.
He yowled quick fury to the world
Till all the hills yelled back;
The top-hawse gave a snort and whirled

19

And Bob caught up the slack.
"Oh, glory be to me," laughs he.
"We hit the glory trail.
No human man as I have read
Darst loop a ragin' lion's head,
Nor ever hawse could drag one dead
Until we told the tale."
'Way high up the Mogollons
That top-hawse done his best,
Through whippin' brush and rattlin' stones,
From canyon-floor to crest.
But ever when Bob turned and hoped
A limp remains to find,
A red-eyed lion, belly roped
But healthy, loped behind.
"Oh, glory be to me" grunts he.
"This glory trail is rough,
Yet even till the Judgment Morn
I'll keep this dally 'round the horn,
For never any hero born
Could stoop to holler: Nuff!"
Three suns had rode their circle home
Beyond the desert's rim,
And turned their star-herds loose to roam
The ranges high and dim;
Yet up and down and 'round and 'cross
Bob pounded, weak and wan,
For pride still glued him to his hawse
And glory drove him on.
"Oh, glory be to me," sighs he.
"He kaint be drug to death,
But now I know beyond a doubt
Them heroes I have read about
Was only fools that stuck it out
To end of mortal breath."
'Way high up the Mogollons
A prospect man did swear
That moon dreams melted down his bones
And hoisted up his hair:
A ribby cow-hawse thundered by,
A lion trailed along,
A rider, ga'nt but chin on high,
Yelled out a crazy song.
"Oh, glory be to me!" cries he,

"And to my noble noose!
Oh, stranger, tell my pards below
I took a rampin' dream in tow,
And if I never lay him low,
I'll never turn him loose!"
[65]

BACON

You're salty and greasy and smoky as sin
But of all grub we love you the best.
You stuck to us closer than nighest of kin
And helped us win out in the West,
You froze with us up on the Laramie trail;
You sweat with us down at Tucson;
When Injun was painted and white man was pale
You nerved us to grip our last chance by the tail
And load up our Colts and hang on.
You've sizzled by mountain and mesa and plain
Over campfires of sagebrush and oak;
The breezes that blow from the Platte to the main
Have carried your savory smoke.
You're friendly to miner or puncher or priest;
You're as good in December as May;
You always came in when the fresh meat had ceased
And the rough course of empire to westward was greased
By the bacon we fried on the way.
We've said that you weren't fit for white men to eat
And your virtues we often forget.
We've called you by names that I darsn't repeat,
But we love you and swear by you yet.
Here's to you, old bacon, fat, lean streak and rin',
All the westerners join in the toast,
From mesquite and yucca to sagebrush and pine,
From Canada down to the Mexican Line,
From Omaha out to the coast!
[67]

THE LOST PARDNER

I ride alone and hate the boys I meet.
Today, some way, their laughin' hurts me so.

21

I hate the mockin'-birds in the mesquite—
And yet I liked 'em just a week ago.
I hate the steady sun that glares, and glares!
The bird songs make me sore.
I seem the only thing on earth that cares
'Cause Al ain't here no more!
'Twas just a stumblin' hawse, a tangled spur—
And, when I raised him up so limp and weak,
One look before his eyes begun to blur
And then—the blood that wouldn't let 'im speak!
And him so strong, and yet so quick he died,
And after year on year
When we had always trailed it side by side,
He went—and left me here!
We loved each other in the way men do
And never spoke about it, Al and me,
But we both *knowed*, and knowin' it so true
Was more than any woman's kiss could be.
We knowed—and if the way was smooth or rough,
The weather shine or pour,
While I had him the rest seemed good enough—
But he ain't here no more!
What is there out beyond the last divide?
Seems like that country must be cold and dim.
He'd miss this sunny range he used to ride,
And he'd miss me, the same as I do him.
It's no use thinkin'—all I'd think or say
Could never make it clear.
Out that dim trail that only leads one way
He's gone—and left me here!
[pg]

"I wait to hear him ridin' up behind."
[pg]

[69]
The range is empty and the trails are blind,
And I don't seem but half myself today.
I wait to hear him ridin' up behind
And feel his knee rub mine the good old way.
He's dead—and what that means no man kin tell.
Some call it "gone before."
Where? I don't know, but God! I know so well

22

That he ain't here no more!
[70]

GOD'S RESERVES

One time, 'way back where the year marks fade,
God said: "I see I must lose my West,
The prettiest part of the world I made,
The place where I've always come to rest,
For the White Man grows till he fights for bread
And he begs and prays for a chance to spread.
"Yet I won't give all of my last retreat;
I'll help him to fight his long trail through,
But I'll keep some land from his field and street
The way that it was when the world was new.
He'll cry for it all, for that's his way,
And yet he may understand some day."
And so, from the painted Bad Lands, 'way
To the sun-beat home of the 'Pache kin,
God stripped some places to sand and clay
And dried up the beds where the streams had been.
He marked His reserves with these plain signs
And stationed His rangers to guard the lines.
Then the White Man came, as the East growed old,
And blazed his trail with the wreck of war.
He riled the rivers to hunt for gold
And found the stuff he was lookin' for;
Then he trampled the Injun trails to ruts
And gashed through the hills with railroad cuts.
He flung out his barb-wire fences wide
And plowed up the ground where the grass was high.
He stripped off the trees from the mountain side
And ground out his ore where the streams run by,
Till last came the cities, with smoke and roar,
And the White Man was feelin' at home once more.
But Barrenness, Loneliness, suchlike things
That gall and grate on the White Man's nerves,
Was the rangers that camped by the bitter springs
And guarded the lines of God's reserves.
So the folks all shy from the desert land,
'Cept mebbe a few that kin understand.
There the world's the same as the day 'twas new,
With the land as clean as the smokeless sky

23

And never a noise as the years have flew,
But the sound of the warm wind driftin' by;
And there, alone, with the man's world far,
There's a chance to think who you really are.
And over the reach of the desert bare,
When the sun drops low and the day wind stills,
Sometimes you kin almost see Him there,
As He sits alone on the blue-gray hills,
A-thinkin' of things that's beyond our ken
And restin' Himself from the noise of men.
[74]

THE MARRIED MAN

There's an old pard of mine that sits by his door
And watches the evenin' skies.
He's sat there a thousand of evenin's before
And I reckon he will till he dies.
El pobre! I reckon he will till he dies,
And hear through the dim, quiet air
Far cattle that call and the crickets that cheep
And his woman a-singin' a kid to sleep
And the creak of her rockabye chair.
Once we made camp where the last light would fail
And the east wasn't white till we'd start,
But now he is deaf to the call of the trail
And the song of the restless heart.
El pobre! the song of the restless heart
That you hear in the wind from the dawn!
He's left it, with all the good, free-footed things,
For a slow little song that a tired woman sings
And a smoke when his dry day is gone.
I've rode in and told him of lands that were strange,
Where I'd drifted from glory to dread.
He'd tell me the news of his little old range
And the cute things his kids had said!
El pobre! the cute things his kids had said!
And the way six-year Billy could ride!
And the dark would creep in from the gray chaparral
And the woman would hum, while I pitied my pal
And thought of him like he had died.
He rides in old circles and looks at old sights
And his life is as flat as a pond.

24

He loves the old skyline he watches of nights
And he don't seem to care for beyond.
El pobre! he don't seem to dream of beyond,
Nor the room he could find, there, for joy.
"Ain't you ever oneasy?" says I one day.
But he only just smiled in a pityin' way
While he braided a quirt for his boy.
He preaches that I orter fold up my wings
And that even wild geese find a nest.
That "woman" and "wimmen" are different things
And a saddle nap isn't a rest.
El pobre! he's more for the shade and the rest
And he's less for the wind and the fight,
Yet out in strange hills, when the blue shadows rise
And I'm tired from the wind and the sun in my eyes,
I wonder, sometimes, if he's right.
I've courted the wind and I've followed her free
From the snows that the low stars have kissed
To the heave and the dip of the wavy old sea,
Yet I reckon there's somethin' I've missed.
El pobre! Yes, mebbe there's somethin' I've missed,
And it mebbe is more than I've won—
Just a door that's my own, while the cool shadows creep,
And a woman a-singin' my kid to sleep
When I'm tired from the wind and the sun.
NOTE.—"El pobre," Spanish, "Poor fellow."
[78]

THE OLD COW MAN

I rode across a valley range
I hadn't seen for years.
The trail was all so spoilt and strange
It nearly fetched the tears.
I had to let ten fences down
(The fussy lanes ran wrong)
And each new line would make me frown
And hum a mournin' song.
Oh, it's squeak! squeak! squeak!
Hear 'em stretchin' of the wire!
The nester brand is on the land;
I reckon I'll retire,
While progress toots her brassy horn

25

And makes her motor buzz,
I thank the Lord I wasn't born
No later than I was.
'Twas good to live when all the sod,
Without no fence nor fuss,
Belonged in pardnership to God,
The Gover'ment and us.
With skyline bounds from east to west
And room to go and come,
I loved my fellow man the best
When he was scattered some.
Oh, it's squeak! squeak! squeak!
Close and closer cramps the wire.
There's hardly play to back away
And call a man a liar.
Their house has locks on every door;
Their land is in a crate.
These ain't the plains of God no more,
They're only real estate.
There's land where yet no ditchers dig
Nor cranks experiment;
It's only lovely, free and big
And isn't worth a cent.
I pray that them who come to spoil
May wait till I am dead
Before they foul that blessed soil
With fence and cabbage head.
Yet it's squeak! squeak! squeak!
Far and farther crawls the wire.
To crowd and pinch another inch
Is all their heart's desire.
The world is overstocked with men
And some will see the day
When each must keep his little pen,
But I'll be far away.
[pg]

"There's land where yet no ditchers dig
Nor cranks experiment;
It's only lovely, free and big
And isn't worth a cent."
[pg]

26

[81]

When my old soul hunts range and rest
Beyond the last divide,
Just plant me in some stretch of West
That's sunny, lone and wide.
Let cattle rub my tombstone down
And coyotes mourn their kin,
Let hawses paw and tromp the moun'
But don't you fence it in!
Oh, it's squeak! squeak! squeak!
And they pen the land with wire.
They figure fence and copper cents
Where we laughed 'round the fire.
Job cussed his birthday, night and morn.
In his old land of Uz,
But I'm just glad I wasn't born
No later than I was!

[82]

THE PLAINSMEN

Men of the older, gentler soil,
Loving the things that their fathers wrought—
Worn old fields of their fathers' toil,
Scarred old hills where their fathers fought—
Loving their land for each ancient trace,
Like a mother dear for her wrinkled face,
Such as they never can understand
The way we have loved you, young, young land!
Born of a free, world-wandering race,
Little we yearned o'er an oft-turned sod.
What did we care for the fathers' place,
Having ours fresh from the hand of God?
Who feared the strangeness or wiles of you
When from the unreckoned miles of you,
Thrilling the wind with a sweet command,
Youth unto youth called, young, young land?

[pg]

"Born of a free, world-wandering race,
Little we yearned o'er an oft-turned sod."

[pg]

[83]
North, where the hurrying seasons changed
Over great gray plains where the trails lay long,
Free as the sweeping Chinook we ranged,
Setting our days to a saddle song.
Through the icy challenge you flung to us,
Through your shy Spring kisses that clung to us,
Following far as the rainbow spanned,
Fiercely we wooed you, young, young land!
South, where the sullen black mountains guard
Limitless, shimmering lands of the sun,
Over blinding trails where the hoofs rang hard,
Laughing or cursing, we rode and won.
Drunk with the virgin white fire of you,
Hotter than thirst was desire of you;
Straight in our faces you burned your brand,
Marking your chosen ones, young, young land.
When did we long for the sheltered gloom
Of the older game with its cautious odds?
Gloried we always in sun and room,
Spending our strength like the younger gods.
By the wild sweet ardor that ran in us,
By the pain that tested the man in us,
By the shadowy springs and the glaring sand,
You were our true-love, young, young land.
When the last free trail is a prim, fenced lane
And our graves grow weeds through forgetful Mays,
Richer and statelier then you'll reign,
Mother of men whom the world will praise.
And your sons will love you and sigh for you,
Labor and battle and die for you,
But never the fondest will understand
The way we have loved you, young, young land.
[86]

THE WESTERNER

My fathers sleep on the sunrise plains,
And each one sleeps alone.
Their trails may dim to the grass and rains,
For I choose to make my own.
I lay proud claim to their blood and name,

28

But I lean on no dead kin;
My name is mine, for the praise or scorn,
And the world began when I was born
And the world is mine to win.
They built high towns on their old log sills,
Where the great, slow rivers gleamed,
But with new, live rock from the savage hills
I'll build as they only dreamed.
The smoke scarce dies where the trail camp lies,
Till the rails glint down the pass;
The desert springs into fruit and wheat
And I lay the stones of a solid street
Over yesterday's untrod grass.
I waste no thought on my neighbor's birth
Or the way he makes his prayer.
I grant him a white man's room on earth
If his game is only square.
While he plays it straight I'll call him mate;
If he cheats I drop him flat.
Old class and rank are a wornout lie,
For all clean men are as good as I,
And a king is only that.
I dream no dreams of a nurse-maid state
That will spoon me out my food.
A stout heart sings in the fray with fate
And the shock and sweat are good.
From noon to noon all the earthly boon
That I ask my God to spare
Is a little daily bread in store,
With the room to fight the strong for more,
And the weak shall get their share.
The sunrise plains are a tender haze
And the sunset seas are gray,
But I stand here, where the bright skies blaze
Over me and the big today.
What good to me is a vague "may be"
Or a mournful "might have been,"
For the sun wheels swift from morn to morn
And the world began when I was born
And the world is mine to win.
[89]

THE WIND IS BLOWIN'

My tired hawse nickers for his own home bars;
A hoof clicks out a spark.
The dim creek flickers to the lonesome stars;
The trail twists down the dark.
The ridge pines whimper to the pines below.
The wind is blowin' and I want you so.

The birch has yellowed since I saw you last,
The Fall haze blued the creeks,
The big pine bellowed as the snow swished past,
But still, above the peaks,
The same stars twinkle that we used to know.
The wind is blowin' and I want you so.

The stars up yonder wait the end of time
But earth fires soon go black.
I trip and wander on the trail I climb—
A fool who will look back
To glimpse a fire dead a year ago.
The wind is blowin' and I want you so.

Who says the lover kills the man in me?
Beneath the day's hot blue
This thing hunts cover and my heart fights free
To laugh an hour or two.
But now it wavers like a wounded doe.
The wind is blowin' and I want you so.

[91]

ON BOOT HILL

Up from the prairie and through the pines,
Over your straggling headboard lines
Winds of the West go by.
You must love them, you booted dead,
More than the dreamers who died in bed—
You old-timers who took your lead
Under the open sky!

Leathery knights of the dim old trail,
Lawful fighters or scamps from jail,
Dimly your virtues shine.
Yet who am I that I judge your wars,
Deeds that my daintier soul abhors,
Wide-open sins of the wide outdoors,
Manlier sins than mine.

30

Dear old mavericks, customs mend.
I would not glory to make an end
Marked like a homemade sieve.
But with a touch of your own old pride
Grant me to travel the trail I ride.
Gamely and gaily, the way you died,
Give me the nerve to live.
Ay, and for you I will dare assume
Some Valhalla of sun and room
Over the last divide.
There, in eternally fenceless West,
Rest to your souls, if they care to rest,
Or else fresh horses beyond the crest
And a star-speckled range to ride.